The Case of the Beagle Burglar

BY **NANCY KRULIK**
ILLUSTRATED BY **GARY LaCOSTE**

SCHOLASTIC INC.

New York   Toronto   London   Auckland
Sydney   Mexico City   New Delhi   Hong Kong

For Pepper, for obvious reasons

ISBN 978-0-545-26654-3

12 11 10 9 8 7 6 5 4 3 2 1   11 12 13 14 15 16/0

Printed in the U.S.A.   40
First printing, July 2011
Book design by Yaffa Jaskoll

Chapter 1

The baseball was soaring right toward me. I was ready. Any second now, I would catch the game-winning ball and . . . Ouch! The ball smacked me right in the head.

I opened my eyes. *Wow. That was so real.* It was like I'd actually been playing professional baseball—which is *totally* my dream. *And* it was like I'd really gotten slammed in the head with a ball—which is totally *not.* I'd had a dream and a nightmare all in one.

My dog, Scout, padded into my room. He stuck his snout near my face and gave me a lick. *Whoa,* did his breath smell. Scout wakes me up that same way every morning. He's like a stinky alarm clock.

Scout really needed to go out. I could tell by the way he was pacing around on his brown and white beagle legs, with his long, floppy ears stiff against his head.

The last thing I wanted to do was clean up beagle pee. I leaped out of bed and looked for my Angels T-shirt.

Only, the shirt wasn't in my drawer. It wasn't anywhere. *This was not good.* I always wear my Angels shirt on Fridays. It's my good-luck-on-the-spelling-quiz shirt.

Scout was circling around and around. I knew I had to hurry. So I threw on my Orioles shirt. It had gotten me a B on my math quiz on Monday. I guessed that would do.

Scout was kind of hungry, like he always is in the morning. So I figured this would be a real quick walk. Number one. Number two. And then back inside for breakfast.

But as soon as Scout and I stepped outside, I saw two squirrels on the lawn. *Uh-oh.* Squirrels meant trouble.

Scout's ears perked up. He'd seen the squirrels, too.

Squeak. Squeal. Squeak. That was the squirrels.

Ruff! Ruff! That was Scout.

"HEY!" That was me shouting as Scout took off after the squirrels, with me on the other end of his leash.

The squirrels ran up the side of an oak tree.

Scout jumped up and down at the base of the tree.

BAM! Something slammed me on the head, hard. It felt kind of like the baseball in my dream. But this thing was real. And it hurt.

Whatever it was hit me so hard it knocked me to the ground. My fingers shook. My toes wiggled. My head buzzed.

A few seconds later, when I opened my eyes, Scout was standing over me.

"Are you okay, Jack?" I heard someone ask me in a low-pitched, dopey kind of voice.

I sat up slowly and looked around. I didn't see anyone except Scout and the two squirrels he'd been chasing.

"Does he *look* okay?" I heard someone with a high voice ask sarcastically.

"I dunno," the dopey voice answered.

"He looks rotten," a second squeaky voice said. "You dogs are so dumb."

"I'm fine," I said. I looked up at the two squirrels. "I just have to catch my breath."

Whoa. Wait a minute. Was I talking to squirrels?

4

I blinked and tried to wake up from this dream. It *had* to be a dream. Just like the baseball one I'd had earlier. Except *this* dream wasn't ending.

"It was those squirrels," Scout told me. "They hit you with an acorn. Squirrels are a real pain in the neck."

"And in the head," I replied. I rubbed the lump on my skull.

Whoa. *Again*. I was talking to my dog. This was no dream. I was *really* talking to Scout. But I couldn't be. That was impossible.

Except it was happening.

My stomach started to feel the way it had that time I ate too many hot dogs and then went on the Double Dip Flip roller coaster. I felt like I was going to puke. *What had happened to me?*

"It wasn't my fault," Scout insisted. "I wouldn't even have been near that tree if Zippy and Zappy hadn't been teasing me." He stopped for a minute. "Hey! I understood every word you just said! How did that happen?"

Funny, I was wondering the same thing.

"I mean, I always understand some things you say, like *out*, or *sit*, or *cookie*, or *good dog*. But now . . ."

"I know," I said. "It's strange. It doesn't sound like you're barking anymore. It's just like you're talking to me. And so are they." I pointed to the squirrels.

"You mean Zippy and Zappy," Scout said. "Zippy's the one with the bite in his ear."

"Hey!" Zippy argued. "Can I help it if I got in a fight with a raccoon?"

"And Zappy's the one with the crooked front tooth," Scout continued.

"Hey!" Zappy said. "They don't make braces for squirrels."

"You guys have *names*?" I asked the squirrels.

"Sure," Zippy said.

"Don't you two-legged animals have names?" Zappy added. That made sense. But it was about the only thing that did. I couldn't believe that I was suddenly talking to animals.

"How did this happen?" I asked.

"I don't know," Zippy said. "Unless . . ."

"Unless what?" I asked him.

Zippy looked at Zappy. "You don't think that old story Grandpa Zoomer told us could be true, do you?"

"What story?" Scout and I both asked at the
same time.

"It was just a silly fairy tale," Zappy said. "He told us
this was a magic tree. Grandpa used to say if you hit a
two-legged big head with an acorn from this tree, he'd
get special powers."

"Like being able to talk to animals?" I asked.

"Maybe," Zappy told me. "Grandpa didn't really say
what kind of special powers."

"I thought it was just some story he told us to get us
to stay in the tree when it was bedtime," Zippy said.
"But it must have been true."

"I guess so," I said. "I mean, you *did* hit me with an acorn from this tree, and I *am* talking to you guys."

"Yeah," Zippy and Zappy said at the same time. "Weird, huh?"

It was weird. Really weird. But kind of cool, too. How many other kids could talk to animals? No one I knew.

Wait until my best friend, Leo, heard about this!

I stopped myself right there. Leo could never hear about this. No one could.

They'd think I was crazy. And I wasn't one hundred percent sure I wasn't.

One thing I *was* sure of was that I was hungry. I had to get moving if I was going to have time to eat breakfast before the school bus came. I stopped talking and yanked Scout back toward the house. I was in a hurry. But I still needed to do one more thing today—change my shirt. The one I had been wearing was all muddy from when I fell on the ground. My mom wouldn't be happy if I tried to go to school with mud on my shirt. So I ran upstairs and quickly put on my Phillies shirt. That shirt had gotten me an A– on my last grammar quiz. I figured I'd need luck like that to get me through today.

Chapter 2

Later that morning, my class was busy doing research in the school library. We were working on plans for our science fair projects. Unfortunately, I was having trouble concentrating, thanks to all the animal chatter going on around me.

No one else in my class could understand animal talk. So they didn't hear the two moths that were flying around the lamp on my table. But I did.

"You're hogging all the light," I heard one moth say. "How am I supposed to get tan? Look at me. I'm white all over."

"We're *supposed* to be white all over," the other moth said. "We're moths."

Just then, Leo sat down next to me. He had a pile of science books in his arms.

9

"You know the grammar quiz isn't until Tuesday, right?" he asked me.

"Yeah," I said. "Why?"

"You're wearing your Phillies shirt," Leo said. "That's your good-luck-on-the-grammar-quiz shirt."

Leo is a great best friend. He keeps track of stuff like that. And he doesn't think I'm weird for having lucky T-shirts.

"My Angels shirt was in the wash," I told him. I looked at his stack of books. "You figure out what you're doing for the science fair?"

"Yeah," Leo said. "I just have to make my list of supplies and draw up the plan." He brushed his hair out of his eyes. Leo's hair is always a curly mess. I don't think he ever combs it. Today he had something fuzzy stuck in it.

I wasn't surprised that Leo already had his science fair idea all planned out. He's really into science. He got a microscope for his birthday, and it's his prized possession. Just like the Derek Jeter rookie baseball card my dad got me for my birthday.

Unfortunately, baseball cards didn't do me any good in school. I was the only kid in the class who didn't know what he was doing for the science fair.

Too bad I didn't have a good-luck-coming-up-with-a-science-project shirt.

"Uh-oh," Leo whispered. "Here comes trouble."

I turned just in time to see Trevor the Terrible coming toward us. That was definitely not good. Trevor was the meanest kid in the third grade. He was also the biggest. Leo was the shortest. So when Trevor was next to Leo, he looked like a mountain. *A mean mountain.*

Trevor plopped himself down in the third chair at our table. "Leo, did you get the answers to five, fourteen, and nineteen on the math homework?" Trevor whispered.

Leo shrugged. "I'm pretty good at math."

"Hand 'em over," Trevor demanded.

Leo didn't say a word. But he didn't reach into his backpack, either. That made Trevor mad.

"Come on, *Cubby*," he said

Cubby was Leo's mom's nickname for him. She called him that because Leo is a lion's name, and lion babies are called cubs. But no guy wants anyone knowing about something like that. Especially not when that someone is Trevor the Terrible. But Trevor had heard Leo's mom call him Cubby once, and that was all it took.

I couldn't imagine what Trevor would do if he found out I'd been talking to animals that morning. *Yikes!* I definitely had to keep that secret!

Leo looked at Trevor. Trevor *glared* at Leo. Leo hesitated. Then he reached into his bag.

"Here," Leo said, pulling out his worksheet. "But what if Mrs. Sloane finds out?"

"She won't," Trevor said. "And besides, she wouldn't be mad. She loves me."

That was true. Trevor was the kind of kid who knew just what to say to a teacher to make her like him. That just made the rest of us kids fear him even more.

"What about when we have a test?" Leo asked him.

"No problem," Trevor told him. "I'll sit next to you. Or the Brainiac."

We all knew who the Brainiac was. Elizabeth Morrison: the smartest girl in the third grade. Leo was good at math and science. But the Brainiac was amazing at everything.

We all looked across the room at Elizabeth. She was busy scribbling notes in her binder. Her hair looked like red, squiggly worms, and she was smiling like this science fair was the greatest thing since Disney World. *Weird.*

Elizabeth looked up. She waved right at me.

Oh man. There's nothing more embarrassing than getting caught staring at someone. Especially when that someone is a weirdo like Elizabeth the Brainiac. She was always smiling at me and doing this batting-her-eyelashes thing. It was creepy.

"One of these days you're going to get caught copying," Leo told Trevor.

"Who's gonna tell?" Trevor asked. *"You?"*

The way Trevor said *you* was scary. Leo and I sunk down in our seats, which only made me feel smaller next to Trevor.

Just then, Mrs. Sloane walked over to our table. Trevor quickly tucked Leo's math sheet into his notebook.

"Hello, Trevor," she said. "I see you've switched tables."

Trevor flashed a big, phony smile. "I've already got my project planned out. But Jack doesn't. I'm helping him brainstorm."

"You're a good friend." Mrs. Sloane smiled at Trevor. Then she frowned at me. "You'd better get on it, Jack. The science fair is next week."

"Yes, ma'am."

As Mrs. Sloane walked away, I stared at Trevor. "Why did you get me in trouble?" I asked him.

Trevor smiled. "Because you make it so easy," he said.

Grrr. Trevor the Terrible had struck again.

Chapter 3

By the end of lunch, I still had no idea what I was going to do for the science fair. So I wasn't in a particularly good mood when I went outside for recess.

Things kept getting worse. I started hearing animals talking again.

"Hup . . . two . . . three . . . four. Hup . . . two . . . three . . . four."

I looked down to see an army of tiny ants marching into an anthill.

"I don't know but I've been told. Anthill Four is really bold," they chanted. *"SOUND OFF. One, two. SOUND OFF. Three, four . . ."*

"Look out above!" one of the ants shouted out suddenly. "Incoming giant foot! Troops, run for cover!"

The ants all scattered out of the way of the huge foot shadow that was looming above them. They escaped just seconds before Leo's sneaker would have squashed them.

"Hey, Jack, you want to play wall ball?" Leo asked as he walked over to me. He held up a yellow tennis ball. "This one's got lots of bounce. I took it out of a fresh can this morning." He started to bounce the ball on the blacktop.

"DON'T!" I shouted.

Leo stared at me. "It's okay. I asked my mom if I could take it."

"No," I said. "I mean *don't bounce it there*. You're gonna squash the anthill."

Leo gave me a weird look. "So what?"

"So what?" I repeated. "But they're . . ." I stopped midsentence. What was I going to say? "It's just that, well, they didn't do anything to us, so why should we do anything to them?"

"That's so sweet, Jack," Elizabeth said.

I looked at her, surprised. "Where did you come from?" I asked.

"From behind that tree," she said with a goofy grin. "I was watching you watch the ants."

Okay, *that* was creepy.

By this time, a crowd had gathered around Elizabeth, Leo, and me.

"In some countries, killing animals—even insects— is considered murder." Elizabeth twirled a curly red hair worm around her finger. "I'm glad you're not a murderer, Jack."

Please stop, I thought.

But Trevor the Terrible had already heard her. "Me, too, Jack," he said in a girly voice. The other kids all laughed.

Trevor was really getting on my nerves. I wished I could stamp him out—just like Leo had almost done to the ant soldiers. But of course I couldn't. Ants were little. Trevor was huge.

"Hey look, it's Big Head." I suddenly heard someone say.

"Hi, Big Head!" Someone else called to me.

I looked up in the tree. There they were. Zippy and Zappy.

Zippy held up an acorn. "Look out below!" he shouted.

Bam! The acorn landed right on my head.

"Gotcha, Big Head," Zippy teased.

"Cut it out!" I shouted.

"What did you say?" Trevor asked. He stood up really, really tall.

I started getting that hot-dogs-on-a-roller-coaster feeling in my stomach again.

"I wasn't talking to you," I said. "I was . . . um . . ." I couldn't tell all these kids about Zippy and Zappy. So instead I said, "I was talking to the Brainiac. She's bugging me."

Elizabeth looked like she'd been punched in the gut. Her eyes got red, and her nose started to run. She wiped her nose with her hand and walked away.

I felt kind of rotten about doing that. But I had no choice. Trevor the Terrible would have teased me for the rest of my life if he knew I was talking to squirrels.

Sorry, Brainiac, I thought to myself. But during recess, it's every man for himself.

Chapter 4

After school, Leo and I headed over to the hardware store. He was going to buy the supplies he needed for his science project. And I was going to look around and hope that something in the store gave me an idea.

But it was hard for me to think about science, or anything else. How's a guy supposed to think when all around him animals are talking?

We were almost at Pig Path Road when I heard a bunch of pigeons arguing over a bagel on the ground.

"That big piece is mine," a brown and white pigeon said, taking a bite.

"I'm always stuck with the burned part," a pigeon with a black spot on his wing said.

"I'm going to a different restaurant," an all-white bird cooed. "There are too many pigeons here."

"You *are* a pigeon," Black Spot reminded her.

"I'm a *dove*," she corrected him.

As she flew off, the spotted bird clucked angrily, "Doves are just pigeons with attitude."

I laughed.

Leo looked at me. "What's so funny?" he asked.

Oops. I'd almost blown it. I couldn't tell Leo about this whole talking-to-animals thing. I didn't want my best friend to think he was hanging out with a crazy person.

"Nothing," I said quickly.

I kept quiet the whole rest of the way. I didn't even mention the baby birds I heard arguing over who had gotten the bigger piece of chewed-up worm, even though I knew Leo loves cool stuff like chewed-up worms. I tried to keep things normal.

"What can I do for you boys?" Mr. Hammersmith asked as Leo and I entered his hardware store.

"A lot," Leo told him. "I'm building a robot for the science fair. I'm going to program it to clean my room."

Ever since I can remember, Leo has been building robots from kits. Most of them just walk around or have flashing lights and voice chips. A cleaner-upper robot was going to take some major work.

Leo pulled a sheet of paper from his backpack. "These are my plans," he said.

"Here, let me see those," Mr. Hammersmith said. "I was interested in robots when I was your age. Made a few myself."

I'd never thought of someone as old as Mr. Hammersmith as having ever been a kid. To me, he'd always been an old guy with hair growing out of his ears who walked with a cane.

"I've made robots from kits," Leo said. "But this time, I'm going to use a kit motor and build the rest myself."

Mr. Hammersmith looked at Leo's list of supplies. "This is pretty impressive," he said. "You're a smart boy."

Huh? I had never heard Mr. Hammersmith give anyone a compliment before. He's usually all business. He must have *really* liked Leo's idea.

"Some of these things are in the back storage closet. I'll get those, and you go get a package of screws and a screwdriver. Third aisle, on the left. Make sure you don't mix up the screws. I've got them divided by size," he added sternly.

Okay, *that* was the Mr. Hammersmith I knew.

"I won't," Leo promised.

As Mr. Hammersmith went off to help Leo, I looked around the store for something that could give me a project idea. But all I saw were nails, hammers, and screwdrivers.

"Hi, Jack."

The voice came out of nowhere. I looked around and came face-to-face with the Brainiac.

Oh man. I wasn't in the mood for Elizabeth's smiling and eyelash batting. Unfortunately, there was no escaping her.

"Hi," I grunted. I looked away. I figured she was pretty mad at me after what I had done to her at recess.

"I bet you're shopping for the science fair," she said. "Unless you don't have an idea yet."

Okay, I was right. She was mad. I could tell because that wasn't the kind of thing the Brainiac usually said to me. And she wasn't batting her eyelashes or twirling her wormy red hair either.

"I'm sorta shopping," I told her. Which was true. I was looking for something. I just didn't know what.

I wanted to get away from Elizabeth. But that wasn't easy. She kept following me around the store.

"What project are you doing?" Elizabeth asked.

I shrugged. "I don't know yet."

Elizabeth shook her wormy red hair. *Ugh*.

"You better hurry," she told me. "There's not a lot of time left."

Gee, tell me something I don't know, I thought. But all I said was, "I gotta go. I hear Leo calling me."

Actually it wasn't Leo I'd heard at all. I heard a voice that sounded like a cat meowing when it talked. I looked in the direction of the voice and spotted a fat, striped, gray cat in the corner of the store. He was staring at what looked like a hole in the bottom of the wall. I figured it had to be a mouse hole.

"Come out, come out, wherever you are!" I heard the cat purr.

"I didn't hear anything," Elizabeth said.

"Well, I have really good hearing," I said. "I hear lots of things other people don't." *That was definitely the truth!*

"Okay," Elizabeth said.

I walked away from her as fast as I could. But no matter which way I turned, there was someone I didn't want to see in Mr. Hammersmith's hardware store.

"Do you and your *girlfriend* do everything together now?"

It was Trevor the Terrible.

"She's not my girlfriend," I insisted.

"She sure seems to be wherever you are," Trevor said.

That was true. But it wasn't like it was my fault.

"I'm here with Leo," I told Trevor.

Trevor looked around. "I don't see him."

"He's probably talking to Mr. Hammersmith," I said. "Leo is making something amazing for the science fair."

"Oh yeah?" Trevor asked. "What is it?"

I figured I'd better not give away Leo's idea to someone like Trevor. So I just said, "It's a surprise. But it's going to blow you away."

"We'll see," Trevor said. "What are you doing?"

Not that question again! I pretended I had no idea what Trevor was talking about.

"Waiting for Leo," I said. "I just told you."

"Here I am," Leo said, popping up behind me. He had a big Hammersmith's Hardware Store bag in his arms, and his backpack strapped across his back.

Just then, I heard talking coming from the corner of the store, where the cat was still sitting and waiting for the mouse to come out of its hole.

"You don't want me. I'm just a small, skinny mouse," I heard a mouse's soft, squeaky voice say to the cat. He sounded really scared.

I knew how that mouse felt. He was a little guy

trapped in a room being threatened by a big bully. Just like Leo and me.

Only, *we* could escape. "Let's get out of here," I told Leo.

"Right behind you," Leo agreed.

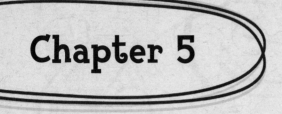

Chapter 5

"Tug-of-war! Let's play tug-of-war!"

Scout dropped a toy at my feet. It was later that afternoon, and Leo and I were playing Space Crusaders, a new video game my uncle had sent me.

"Not now," I told Scout. "Leo and I are playing. I'll play with you later."

"You always say 'later,'" Scout insisted.

"I do not *always* say 'later,'" I said.

Leo laughed. "It's like you two are actually having a conversation."

Oops. I'd completely forgotten that I was talking to my dog. To Leo, it just sounded like Scout was barking. I was going to have to watch that.

"I just know what his different barks mean," I said.

Then I knocked two aliens off the screen. "Oh yeah! Space Crusader to the rescue!"

"What's that smell?" Scout asked. He was sniffing around. "*Mmm . . .* baloney!"

"Get your dog out of my backpack," Leo said.

"He smells food," I told him. "Did you leave part of your sandwich in there?"

Leo shrugged. "I don't know. He's pulling out my calculator. I don't want dog slobber on it."

"Scout, get out," I said, taking the calculator and wiping the dog slime on my shirt. "Leo and I are busy."

Leo laughed. "Like he's gonna understand that," he said.

I frowned. Leo might have been great at math and science, but when it came to talking to animals, I understood plenty.

Leo was the one who didn't.

Part of me really wanted to tell Leo what was going on. I mean, he was my best friend. Well, my best *human* friend. But I didn't know how long my new ability would last. It could be gone tomorrow. So what was the point in telling Leo? He might think I was crazy.

Just then, my mom poked her head into my room. "Leo, your mom's here," she said.

"Can I have five more minutes?" Leo asked. "I've almost captured Jack's spaceship."

"Not today," my mother told him. "Your mom has two stops to make on the way home. She needs you to go now."

And that was it. Even if I'd wanted to tell Leo, I couldn't do it now.

That's my favorite kind of decision. The kind you don't have to make for yourself.

"Hey, Jack, okay if I stop by and get my robot plans tomorrow morning?" Leo asked me that night on the phone.

"I don't have your plans," I told him.

"But they have to be at your house," Leo insisted. "They were in my backpack, and now they're not."

"I never even saw them," I told Leo. "Check again."

"They're not there," Leo said. "The only thing in there is my notebook, the receipt from the hardware store, and a slimy calculator." He stopped for a minute. "Your dog was poking around in my backpack. I bet he ate them!"

"Why would Scout eat your robot plans?" I asked.

"Your dog will eat anything," Leo said. "Remember the time he grabbed the steak before the Fourth of July barbecue? Or when he ate your sister's ice-cream cake at her birthday party?"

How could I forget? My sister, Mia, had cried for an hour. She was five now, but she still acted like a baby sometimes.

"Those were *foods*," I pointed out. "Why would a dog eat paper?"

"Dogs are always eating homework," Leo insisted.

"But . . ." I started.

"Now I won't have a project for the science fair because of your stupid dog," Leo said.

"My dog is NOT stupid," I shouted. "And anyway, why can't you just do the plans over again?"

"Because it takes too long," Leo said. "The robot's really complicated. The science fair is next Friday. I don't have time to plan the whole thing again."

"Well, Scout didn't do it," I said. "He isn't a thief!"

At the sound of his name, Scout came running into my room. He leaped up on my bed and barked.

"That sounded like a confession," Leo said.

"Shows what you know," I told Leo. "He said, 'Let's play fetch.'"

"Oh, right," Leo said. "So you speak dog now?"

I sure wasn't going to tell Leo what had happened to me now. Not after what he'd just said about Scout.

"You can play fetch with your dumb dog all you want," Leo told me. "*I'm* not playing with you until I get my plans back."

"Fine!" I said. I slammed down the phone.

Except it wasn't fine at all. It was rotten.

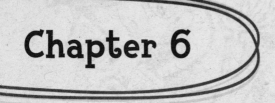

Chapter 6

At first, I was really mad at Leo. He was the one who lost his stupid robot plans. Why was he blaming Scout?

But then I thought about it. Scout had been known to chew up a lot of stuff. Half my socks had holes in them because of his chewing. And Mia's baby doll did have one pretty chewed-up arm, thanks to Scout using it to play fetch. So it was possible. . . .

No! No way!

I reached down and scratched Scout on his belly—right on that special spot that makes his leg move up and down.

"A little to the left," Scout said. "Yeah, there. Perfect."

I barely even jumped when Scout started talking to me. *Am I getting used to this whole animal-talking thing?*

"Ouch!"

That was a new voice. A squeaky, little, high-pitched voice.

"Stop scratching," the voice said. "Fleas have very delicate skin."

"I gotta give you a flea bath," I told Scout.

"You're telling me," Scout answered.

"You didn't eat Leo's robot plans, did you, boy?" I asked as I scratched.

Scout's leg stopped moving. He rolled over and stared at me.

"I can't believe you asked me that," he growled. "I don't eat homework. I eat food."

"And socks and dolls," I reminded him.

Scout's ears flattened and his tail drooped. His eyes opened wide, and he raised his lip so I could see his teeth. Then he raced out of my room.

I was in the kitchen making a snack when my mom brought Scout in from his evening walk.

"I don't know what's with Scout tonight," my mom said. "The minute we got outside, he started howling, like he was mad at the moon."

I frowned. Scout was mad, all right. He was mad at *me*.

Great. Now my best friend and my dog were both mad at me. How rotten was that?

But by the next morning, Scout seemed to be back to his old self. He licked my face to wake me up.

"Get up," he urged. "I gotta go out."

"I'm coming." I rolled out of bed and threw on my nothing-to-do-on-a-Saturday Mets T-shirt. Then I ran downstairs, got Scout's leash, and took him outside.

"Aahhh," Scout sighed as he let out a long pee on a fire hydrant. "That's better."

Nobody was around, so I figured it was safe to talk to Scout. "I'm sorry I thought you ate Leo's homework," I said.

Scout looked up and gave me a smile—the kind where his tongue hangs out so far that he starts to drool. "It's okay," he said. "We're pals. But you owe me a treat when we get home."

I gave him a kid smile. The kind where my mouth is shut so I *don't* drool. "You got it."

We walked a little farther. Then Scout stopped to talk to one of his dog friends.

"Hey, Biscuit," Scout greeted a brown and white boxer who was sitting on his lawn. He sniffed Biscuit's butt.

"Hey, Scout," Biscuit said, taking a sniff. "What's happening?"

"Just taking a walk," Scout answered.

Biscuit looked up at me and growled. "What's the traitor doing here?"

Scout rolled around on the grass. "I need someone on the other side of the leash."

"I'm not a traitor," I said. And I knew it was the truth. But for some reason, the way Biscuit was staring at me, I almost felt like one.

I wished there was some way to prove to Scout, Biscuit, and any other dog in the neighborhood that I was on their side. But I didn't know what to do to show Biscuit I believed Scout. I mean, it wasn't like I was about to sniff Scout's butt or anything.

There's only so much a guy's willing to do for a friend.

Chapter 7

I tried to pull Scout away from Biscuit, but he wasn't going anywhere. He was with his buddy, and that's where he was going to stay.

I didn't want to make Scout mad again. So I just had to stand there and take whatever Biscuit dished out, while Scout circled around, raised his leg, and peed on the begonias in Biscuit's front lawn.

"We're tired of being blamed for every chewed sock, scratched door, stolen steak, and everyone's missing homework," Biscuit explained to me.

"But you guys *do* chew socks, scratch doors, and steal steak," I said.

"Who are you talking to, Jack?"

I jumped suddenly as a new voice joined the

conversation. It wasn't a dog voice. It was something much worse . . . an *Elizabeth* voice.

Why is Elizabeth showing up wherever I am?

"It sounded like you were talking to those dogs," Elizabeth said.

"What are you doing here?" I asked her. "You don't live on this block."

"I was bird-watching in the park," Elizabeth told me. "It was great. I saw a rose-breasted grosbeak. My first one ever."

I tried hard not to laugh. Elizabeth got excited about the weirdest things.

"But you didn't answer my question," she continued.

Oh man. This was bad. *Really* bad. Elizabeth seemed excited about catching me talking to dogs. She had the same smile on her face that she'd had in the library. It was like I was some sort of science project.

That got me thinking. What if she decided to change her project for the science fair? What if instead of whatever she had planned on making, she did her presentation on kids who talk to animals? Then everyone in school would know about me!

I was starting to feel really sick, so I sat down on a nearby bench. Elizabeth sat right next to me.

"Are you an animal psychic, Jack?" Elizabeth asked. She didn't wait for an answer. She just kept talking. "I've never known anyone who could talk to animals before. I've read about them in books, but I've never seen one in action. It's a very unique talent and . . ."

Elizabeth was still blabbing, but all I could think about was what would happen if Trevor found out about this. He'd tell everyone. I'd be an international freak of nature.

Somehow, Elizabeth seemed to understand. She smiled at me. "Don't worry. I won't say a word," she said. "It's our secret."

The Brainiac and I had a secret. *Oh, man. This is bad.*

Still, I was glad Elizabeth had told me that other people were able to understand what animals were saying. I wondered if they'd been hit by magic acorns, too.

"So, what are you guys talking about?" Elizabeth asked me.

At first I thought about denying it. But I didn't. Maybe I felt bad about making fun of her during recess. Or maybe I wanted to hear more about other people who could talk to animals. So I told her the truth.

"Leo accused Scout of eating his robot plans for the science fair," I said. "Scout says he didn't, but Leo thinks he did."

"And he's going to keep thinking that unless we solve this mystery," Elizabeth said.

"What mystery?" I asked.

"The mystery of the missing homework," Elizabeth answered. "Don't you read mystery books?"

I shook my head. The only kind of books I read for fun are sports books.

"Don't worry," she said. "We'll solve this case."

"What do you mean 'we'?" I repeated.

"You need me," Elizabeth said. "I'm very good at solving mysteries. Usually I just have to read a few chapters to know who did it."

Oh man. First I lose my best friend, and now Elizabeth was telling me I needed her.

Even worse, it was the truth. I didn't know the first thing about solving mysteries. But Elizabeth did. If I had any chance of getting Leo back as a best friend, I was going to have to work with her.

"Okay, you can help," I said finally. "But you can't tell anyone."

"I won't," Elizabeth said with a smile. "It'll be our *second* secret."

"Oh brother," I muttered under my breath.

All of a sudden, Scout started jumping up and down and wagging his tail. "JACK'S GOT A GIRLFRIEND! JACK'S GOT A GIRLFRIEND!" he shouted.

Scout couldn't understand what the Brainiac was saying, but he could tell from the way she acted that she liked me. But that did *not* mean I liked her back!

"I do not!" I told him.

Scout laughed so hard he snorted.

"You 'do not' what?" Elizabeth asked me.

Oh yeah, right. Like I was going to tell her what Scout had just said.

I changed the subject instead. "How do we solve this mystery?" I asked her.

"We start by interviewing anyone who might have seen the crime," she said. "Just wait until I get my pen and notebook out."

I tried not to laugh as Elizabeth pulled a rope, a bottle of water, a swim cap, a Ping-Pong paddle, and, finally, a pen and a notebook out of her backpack.

"What's all that junk for?" I asked.

"You never know what's going to happen," she explained. "I like to be prepared."

I couldn't imagine when anyone would need rope, water, a swim cap, and a Ping-Pong paddle, but that wasn't the mystery we were solving now.

"You can start interviewing the dogs now," Elizabeth told me.

As long as I was here, and Elizabeth already knew I could talk to dogs, I figured it couldn't hurt.

"Did you guys see Leo yesterday?" I asked.

"He was at our house," Scout told me.

"Other than at our house," I said, rolling my eyes. "We already know he was there."

"I was just trying to help," Scout said. "Sheesh."

"I saw Leo on Pig Path Road yesterday. He was talking to some guy with little ears," Biscuit told me.

"Now that's a clue!" I shouted excitedly. I turned to Elizabeth. "Write that down."

"Write what down?" Elizabeth asked. "All I heard was *'ruff, ruff, arroo!'*"

"Biscuit saw Leo talking to some guy with little ears," I translated. "They were on Pig Path Road."

"It's not much to go on," she said. "We need more information."

Just then, Biscuit's owner, Charlie, poked his head out the front door. "Biscuit, food!" he called out.

Biscuit raced into his house without even saying good-bye.

I turned to Elizabeth. "I told you they weren't going to be much help."

"They gave us one clue," Elizabeth noted. "We just need some more pieces of the puzzle."

I hoped she was right. Right now I should have been tossing a ball around with Leo. But instead, I was talking to dogs and hanging out with the Brainiac. This was not my idea of a good way to spend a Saturday.

Chapter 8

Elizabeth and I walked Scout back to my house. We sat down under the oak tree in my front yard and tried to figure this thing out.

"We have to go over all the clues," Elizabeth said. "Did Scout take anything out of Leo's backpack?"

"Just a calculator," I said. "But I got it out of his mouth and put it back, and he swears he didn't take anything else," I told Elizabeth.

"I believe him." Elizabeth petted Scout on the head. "But someone took the plans."

"Maybe it was her," Scout suggested. He pushed his snout toward the far side of the lawn, where a slinky gray cat was happily licking her paws. "There's something really sneaky about Shadow."

"Just ignore her," I told Scout. "She has nothing to do with this."

"*Ignore* me?" Elizabeth asked angrily. "I'm the only one here who knows how to solve a mystery, remember?"

"I wasn't talking about you," I explained. "I was talking about that cat over there."

"She looks sweet," Elizabeth said.

"Did she say 'treat'?" Scout barked excitedly.

Treat was one of the human words Scout understood no matter who said it. But that wasn't what Elizabeth had said. Sometimes Scout only heard what he wanted to hear.

"Sorry, Scout," I explained. "Elizabeth says Shadow looks *sweet.*"

Scout gave me a funny look. "I thought you said this girl was smart."

"Where else did Leo go with that backpack?" Elizabeth asked impatiently.

"School, his house, the hardware store, here," I replied.

"You want to play ball, Jack?" Scout asked suddenly. He was jumping up and down. "I see a ball in the bushes."

I shook my head. "Not now, Old Stinky Breath."

Suddenly, Scout stopped jumping and barking.

"I don't think dog breath stinks at all," he told me.

"What would you expect from someone who says hello by sniffing butts?" Shadow, the gray cat from next door, purred. She began to slink her way over to us.

"At least I don't bathe in spit," Scout told Shadow.

"It's called grooming." Shadow licked her paw.

"Grooming in *spit*," Scout growled.

"He's got you there, Shadow," I said with a laugh.

"Jack, come on," Elizabeth said. She sounded annoyed. "I can't understand Scout and Shadow, remember? If you don't tell me what they're saying, I can't help you. And if I don't help you, you'll never solve this mystery."

Elizabeth was acting like such a know-it-all. But she was right. There was no way I could find Leo's plans on my own.

"Okay," Elizabeth said. "Now, you're sure you and Leo didn't go anywhere else?"

"I'm sure," I said. "We only went to the hardware store and here."

"Wait a minute," Shadow interrupted. "Wasn't Leo carrying one of those delicious frozen creams when you got to the house?"

Wow! Leave it to a cat to remember ice cream. "Oh yeah," I told Elizabeth. "We stopped at Heavenly Scoops before we came here. But Leo didn't open his backpack. We just got the cones and came right here."

"Someone could have slipped the plans out of his backpack without him noticing," Elizabeth said. She wrote *Heavenly Scoops* on her list. "I figure the crime happened somewhere on Pig Path Road, since that seems to be the only place other than here that Leo went."

"But who on Pig Path Road could have done it?" I asked her.

"That boxer said he saw Leo talking to someone with little ears on Pig Path Road," Elizabeth said. "Who do we know with little ears?"

"My sister Mia's friend Sam has little ears," I said.

"Was Sam on Pig Path Road when you were?" Elizabeth asked me.

I shook my head.

"Then he can't be a suspect," she said. "A suspect is someone who had the opportunity to steal the plans.

And someone who had a reason to steal them. That's called the motive."

Boy, what a know-it-all.

"I know what a motive is," I told her. "It was on our vocabulary list, remember?"

"Of course *I* remember," she said. "I just wasn't sure you would."

"Okay, *Brainiac*," I said, using the nickname just because I knew it would make Elizabeth mad. "If you're so smart, who would have a motive to steal Leo's plans?"

Elizabeth shrugged. "It would have to be someone really stupid. Using someone else's plans would be cheating. If you got caught, you'd get an F."

Cheating. That was it! I knew exactly who had stolen the plans. And I'd figured it out before the Brainiac!

"I know someone who had an opportunity *and* a motive," I said.

"Who?" Elizabeth asked.

"Tell us! Tell us!" Scout barked.

"Trevor," I said. "He cheats all the time. And he was at the hardware store."

"But how would he know Leo had the plans with him?" Elizabeth asked me.

I looked down at the ground. That one was my fault. "I told him Leo was doing a great project, and we were there buying supplies for it."

Elizabeth wrote that down.

"Trevor's got a big head," I continued. "It makes his ears look small. Just like Biscuit said."

Elizabeth laughed. "He does have a massive head," she agreed.

"So we've solved the mystery?" I asked excitedly.

"Not exactly," Elizabeth said. "We still have one more thing to do."

"What's that?" I wondered.

"We have to interrogate the suspect," she said. She sounded very official—almost like a real detective.

Uh-oh. I knew that meant I was going over to Trevor the Terrible's house—with only Elizabeth the Brainiac to protect me.

"It won't be so bad," Elizabeth told me.

I gulped. That's what people always say in movies—right before the bad guy leaps out of the basement and gets them!

This was going to be bad. I just knew it.

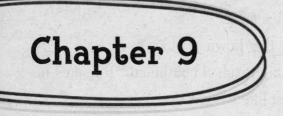

Chapter 9

"Hi, is Trevor home?" Elizabeth asked Trevor's mom as she opened the door that would lead to our doom.

"Sure," his mom said. "He's in the kitchen working on his science project."

His project! Yeah, right. Trevor was working on *Leo's* project. No matter how scared I felt, I wasn't turning back. I had to catch Trevor, for Leo's sake.

We followed Trevor's mom toward the back of the house. Suddenly, we heard someone singing, *badly*.

"You are my sunshine. My only sunshine . . ."

Was that an animal? I didn't think Trevor had a pet.

"You make me happy when skies are gray . . ."

No. It was definitely a human voice. *Trevor's* voice. But why was Trevor singing?

"Trevor, you have company," his mom said as we walked into the kitchen.

Trevor stopped singing. He didn't look happy to see us. I didn't blame him. We were *about* to catch him cheating. And we'd *already* caught him singing.

"I'll leave you kids alone," Trevor's mom said.

I didn't want her to go. Trevor would be nicer with his mom around. But it was too late. She was gone. It was just Trevor the Terrible, the Brainiac, and me.

"What do you two kissy faces want?" Trevor asked us.

That was why I didn't want to spend my Saturday with Elizabeth. The last thing I needed was people thinking I liked her. I had to set Trevor straight. *Now.*

"We are not kissy faces!" I shouted. "We're . . . uh . . . detectives!"

Trevor started to laugh. "Yeah, right. Where are your magnifying glasses and flashlights?"

"Jack and I have *special* investigative tools," Elizabeth told him.

I was impressed. *Investigative tools.* That sounded really cool and detectivelike. Much better than saying, "Some dog said you had small ears." Which I would never say to anyone—especially Trevor!

"Your mom said you were working on your science project," Elizabeth said. She looked around the kitchen. "All I see are a bunch of plants."

"And all I *heard* was your singing," I added.

Trevor turned red. I could tell he hadn't wanted anyone to hear him singing.

"That's my project," he told us. "I'm singing to *some* plants and not to others. I'm trying to figure out if music helps plants grow faster."

Trevor's lousy singing would probably *kill* plants, but I didn't say that. You don't say things like that to a kid like Trevor.

"And you came up with your project on your own?" Elizabeth asked him.

Whoa. It was pretty brave of the Brainiac to just come out and ask.

Trevor definitely didn't like it. He stood up taller so he towered over us. Then he squeezed his lips together really tight. His eyes closed into angry slits.

I could feel my hands starting to sweat.

"Why? Did somebody say I didn't?" Trevor bunched his hands into fists.

I couldn't tell if he was going to hit us or just stand there looking scary, but I started backing toward the door just in case.

"No," I told him. "Nobody said anything about you."

That was the truth. No one had actually said Trevor had stolen Leo's robot plans. Biscuit had just said Leo talked to someone with small ears. And I had only said that Trevor had cheated off of Leo before. That had made Trevor a suspect. But it wasn't enough to convict him.

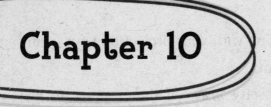

Chapter 10

"Trevor definitely had a good alibi," Elizabeth said as we walked back to my house from Trevor's.

"A good *what*?" I asked her.

"Alibi," Elizabeth repeated. "It's an explanation that proves you're not guilty. And since Trevor isn't making a robot, we can assume he's not the thief."

"Which means we're back at the beginning." I was in a rotten mood. And not just because Trevor had turned out to be innocent. I was mad because he had an idea for his science project. So did Elizabeth. And once we found Leo's plans, he would, too. That left me as the only one without a clue as to what I was going to do.

"Dig, dig, dig. Digging all day long. That's why I sing a digging song."

Suddenly, I heard someone singing. Oh no! Was Trevor the Terrible following us? Quickly, I looked around.

But Trevor wasn't there. And the sound wasn't coming from behind us. It was coming from below.

"*Dig, dig, dig. Deep into the ground. Turn that dirt into a mound.*"

I spotted a mound of dirt on a nearby lawn. It wasn't Trevor singing after all. It was a mole.

"I was sure it was Trevor," Elizabeth continued. "He has such small ears."

"Yeah," I agreed. "Of course, compared to Biscuit and Scout, everyone has small ears. Dog ears are mostly long and floppy."

"You're right," Elizabeth said. "Animals see things differently than we do."

"Yeah, and it's not just dogs," I told Elizabeth. "I saw these pigeons yesterday. They were talking about being at a restaurant. To me, it just looked like they were pecking at a bagel on the sidewalk. But to them, a restaurant was any place to eat."

"Exactly," Elizabeth said.

"So basically, someone with small ears can be any human," I continued. "Or it could be a dog with small ears. "

Elizabeth nodded and hit herself on the forehead. "I wish I'd figured that out sooner."

We were back at my house now. I wasn't feeling any better than I'd been when we left. We still had no idea who had stolen Leo's plans. Worse yet, we didn't have any suspects. Unless . . .

I stared at Elizabeth. "You know, *you* were on Pig Path Road yesterday," I pointed out.

Elizabeth stared at me, surprised. "Are you kidding?" she asked. "Why would *I* steal Leo's plans? I already have an idea for a project."

Hmm . . . What reason *would* the smartest girl in the school have for stealing Leo's plans?

"You always want to have the best project," I realized.

"I always *do*," she corrected me.

"But this time, Leo had a plan for a great project," I said. "Maybe you were eliminating the competition."

"Good thinking," Elizabeth told me.

I smiled proudly.

"Except for one thing," she added.

My smile drooped.

"I never saw Leo," Elizabeth said. "You told me you heard him calling you. I didn't even hear his voice. I never got close enough to him to steal anything."

Bummer. The Brainiac had outsmarted me again.

"You're right," I said. "Sorry."

"Don't be," Elizabeth said. "You were thinking like a detective. That's the only way to solve a mystery."

But even the Brainiac wasn't going to be able to solve a mystery with no clues. "I guess we're never going to find out who stole Leo's homework," I told her.

Just then, Scout ran toward us, his tongue hanging excitedly out of his mouth. "Did you catch the thief?" he asked.

I shook my head. "Sorry, Scout. It wasn't Trevor. And he was our best suspect. Actually, he was our *only* suspect."

Scout buried his head in his paws. His ears and tail drooped.

"Someone else must have seen Leo on Pig Path Road," Elizabeth said.

"Well, if they did, they're not talking," I said.

Elizabeth looked at me kind of funny. I hoped she wasn't going to start batting her eyelashes again.

Luckily, she didn't. She just said, "The witnesses might not be talking to most people. But they will talk to *you*."

Huh? I couldn't understand half the things the Brainiac said.

Elizabeth sighed like she couldn't believe how stupid I was. "Don't you get it? There are always dogs walking on Pig Path Road. One of them must have seen Leo's plans being stolen. You just have to find a dog who saw the thief in action."

"Why would someone steal with a dog right there?" I asked. "Thieves don't want witnesses."

Elizabeth shot me her annoying know-it-all smile. "People figure animals can't say anything even if they *do* see something. The bad guys don't know about people who can talk to animals."

Okay, so maybe she *did* know it all. But that didn't make her any less annoying.

"We have to go where the dogs go," Elizabeth told me. "The dog park."

Scout's ears perked up. *Park* was one of the words he understood no matter who said it.

"I like that girl," Scout barked. "She's smart."

The Brainiac was definitely smart. And she was good at mysteries. But *I* was the one who was going to have to talk to a bunch of animals in the middle of a dog park.

Sure, the Brainiac and Scout were both smiling. They weren't the ones who were about to make fools out of themselves in front of strangers. Unfortunately, that person was me.

Chapter 11

There were a whole lot of people in the dog park when we got there. I knew every one of them would think I was nuts if they saw me talking to a bunch of dogs. And I didn't need any more people making fun of me. I got enough of that from Trevor.

"I can't talk to the dogs here," I told Elizabeth. "These people will think I'm crazy."

"*You* don't have to talk to the dogs, Jack," Elizabeth said. "*Scout* will talk to the dogs. You'll just listen."

As I unclipped Scout's leash, I looked around to make sure no one would hear me talking to him. Then I whispered, "Go find out if any of those dogs saw anyone taking anything from Leo."

Just then, some guy threw a Frisbee. Scout leaped up excitedly.

"Frisbee!" Scout barked. He ran off.

Elizabeth and I watched as Scout leaped up and tried to beat another dog to the Frisbee. But the other dog sprung up faster and gripped it in her mouth.

I shook my head. Scout had the attention span of a flea. He'd run off the minute he smelled a hot dog on the ground, or saw a ball go flying by. Dogs just aren't made to be detectives. There was no way this was going to work. We weren't getting Leo's plans back. He was going to be mad at me forever.

"I bet Scout gets us a lot of clues," Elizabeth said.

"Doubt it," I muttered under my breath. Elizabeth might know a lot about solving mysteries, but I knew a lot about dogs. If you asked me, all Scout was getting was a couple of good sniffs of other dogs' butts.

A few minutes later, Scout padded back to where Elizabeth and I were sitting.

"Okay, see that dog over there, the one with the really long tail?" Scout asked.

I looked over toward the water bowl in the middle of the dog run. There was a brown and white dog with big floppy ears and a really long, fluffy tail.

"Yeah," I said quietly, so only Scout and Elizabeth could hear me.

"Well, he was walking his human on Pig Path Road when . . ."

"Wait a minute," I stopped him. "Who was walking who?"

"He was walking his human," Scout repeated. "What? You thought it was the other way around? Are you kidding? *I'm* the one walking in front. And *you're* the one stuck picking up the poop."

It was hard to argue with logic like that.

"He says he saw Leo through the window of some store near the yellow bathroom on Pig Path Road," Scout continued. "Leo was talking to some guy with three legs."

"*Three legs?*" I repeated. "That dog's crazy. There isn't a person in the world like that."

"What's he saying?" Elizabeth asked me in a voice that was louder than it should have been.

A few people turned around to look at us.

"Wait until we get out of the dog park," I whispered to her.

Elizabeth nodded. "Gotcha."

Elizabeth and I walked Scout—or maybe he walked us—out of the dog park. When we got to a quiet spot, I told Elizabeth, "Scout says a dog saw Leo near the yellow bathroom on Pig Path Road."

"Heavenly Scoops has a yellow bathroom," Elizabeth said. "But how would a dog know about that? Dogs aren't allowed in ice-cream shops."

Still, Elizabeth wrote down the clue. She stared at it for a minute. "This doesn't make any sense," she said.

"Wait, it gets weirder," I said. "The dog said Leo was talking to some guy with three legs."

"That *really* doesn't make any sense," Elizabeth said.

Elizabeth chewed at the end of her pen. I could tell she was mad that she was having trouble with this mystery. Any other time, I would be happy that something had stumped the Brainiac. But not today.

"I think we should go over to Pig Path Road now," Elizabeth said finally.

Elizabeth seemed pretty sure of herself. So I did the only thing I could do. I followed her. I figured if anybody could find a guy with three legs who hung out near a yellow bathroom, it was the Brainiac.

Because it sure wasn't me.

Chapter 12

"A fire hydrant?" I asked Elizabeth as she and I stopped outside Heavenly Scoops a few minutes later. Then I thought about it. Elizabeth was right. The hydrant was yellow. To a dog, this *was* a bathroom.

Just then, a cocker spaniel walked over to Elizabeth and me. "Is this a line for the bathroom?" he asked me. "Can I cut in front of you? Please?"

"When you gotta go, you gotta go," I said. I moved out of the way.

I had to hand it to Elizabeth. She wasn't just a human genius. She was a dog genius, too.

Except for one thing.

"How could a hydrant steal homework?" I asked her.

Elizabeth rolled her eyes and shook her head. She sighed. "The *hydrant* didn't steal anything. Someone who was around here when Leo was did. Someone with three legs."

Now it was *my* turn to sigh. *A man with three legs.* You didn't have to be a Brainiac to know that was impossible. "Will you get serious?" I asked.

But apparently Elizabeth *was* serious. She had her notebook and pen all ready to take notes. "We have to interview people to find out if they saw anything. Where should we start?" she asked.

I didn't have to think hard about that. "Heavenly Scoops," I suggested.

"You remember seeing someone there?" Elizabeth asked hopefully.

"No. But I could use a vanilla cone."

Okay, now Elizabeth looked *really* mad. She shook her head and her red squiggly worm hair bounced all around. "We have more important things to worry about than food, Jack."

I couldn't help it. I love ice cream.

"You're back again," the guy behind the ice-cream counter said as we walked in. He didn't sound happy to see me. Hmmm . . . I wondered why. Could *he* be the thief?

Elizabeth looked over the counter and read his name tag. "Hello, Albert," she said. "You remember Jack?"

"It's hard to forget a kid who samples seven flavors and then decides on vanilla," Albert said with a frown.

Oh, so that was why he was sorry to see me!

I really had done that. It's a trick I learned. You get almost a whole extra scoop by the time you try all those free samples.

"Do you remember anything else about yesterday?" Elizabeth asked Albert. "Like the kid who was with Jack?"

"Yeah. He got a strawberry cone with sprinkles," Albert answered.

"Was there anyone else in here at the same time?" Elizabeth asked.

Albert thought for a minute. "A lady with a baby came in just as they were leaving."

"A lady with a baby," Elizabeth repeated as she scribbled on her notebook. "Did that lady happen to have three legs?"

"Is this some sort of joke?" Albert asked her. He looked around. "Am I on TV?"

"No, I need to know," Elizabeth told him.

"Are you guys gonna order ice cream or what?" Albert asked. I could tell he was tired of answering weird questions.

Elizabeth stuck her notebook back in her backpack. "I doubt a mom would take the time to go into Leo's backpack. She'd be too busy watching the baby," she said. "Come on, Jack. We've learned all we can here."

"But I didn't get my ice cream," I said.

Elizabeth shot me a look. I wasn't going to be sampling any flavors today. I followed her back out onto the sidewalk.

Elizabeth looked into the windows of the nearby stores—the Sealed With a Kiss card shop, the Thai Tanic Asian restaurant, the Sofa So Good furniture store, and Mr. Hammersmith's hardware store.

Elizabeth chewed on her pen for a minute. "Three legs," she muttered. Suddenly, her eyes grew wide. A big smile formed on her lips. "Aha!" she exclaimed "Now I understand exactly what that dog meant!"

"Well, that makes one of us," I said. "I still don't get it."

Elizabeth charged toward Mr. Hammersmith's store

with her nose pointed straight ahead. She looked like a redheaded dog following a scent.

I had no idea what she was up to. I'd figured out how to think like a dog. But I still had no idea how to think like a Brainiac.

There was only one way to find out what Elizabeth had in mind. I had to follow her and hope she knew what she was doing. Because if she didn't, we could be in big trouble.

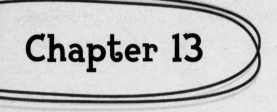

Chapter 13

Mr. Hammersmith was at the cash register when we came in. When he saw us, he limped over.

Elizabeth pointed to his cane. "See?" she whispered. "Three legs."

I had to admit it. Elizabeth was right. To a dog, a cane *would* seem like a third leg. But still . . .

"Mr. Hammersmith?" I began. "Why would a grown-up —"

But Elizabeth shot me a look that shut me up quick. She obviously didn't want Mr. Hammersmith to hear me say he could have stolen Leo's plans. Not yet, anyway.

"What can I do for you kids?" Mr. Hammersmith asked. "More materials for your science fair projects?"

"We don't need anything for our projects," Elizabeth told him. "But Leo does."

Mr. Hammersmith looked around quickly. "Leo? Where is he?"

A bead of sweat formed on Mr. Hammersmith's forehead. It ran down between his eyes and onto his nose. And then it dripped to the floor.

"It's raining!" a voice shouted. "Anyone got an umbrella?"

I looked down just as a cockroach scurried under a stack of wood.

"Leo's not here," Elizabeth replied. "We're helping him."

"I don't understand," Mr. Hammersmith said nervously.

"We're . . . um . . ." It was hard for me to get the words out. I'd never accused a grown-up of stealing before. But I had to, for Leo. "We're looking for Leo's science fair plans."

"They aren't here," Mr. Hammersmith said quickly . . . a little *too* quickly.

Elizabeth began to walk around the store. She stopped at a table with a motor and some wires on it.

"Well, well. What do we have here?" She sounded a lot like a TV detective. "A motor from a kit kids use to make robots. Now why would a grown-up have something like that?"

"It has nothing to do with Leo!" Mr. Hammersmith breathed heavily. "I've wasted enough time on you two. Now get out of here."

But Elizabeth wasn't going anywhere. "We're not leaving without Leo's plans," she told him.

"This is *my* robot," Mr. Hammersmith insisted angrily. "I've been working on it for months. I can prove it. I have a letter from a toy company. They were interested in my robot way before your science fair was announced."

"I'd like to see that letter," Elizabeth told him.

"It's in the back," Mr. Hammersmith said. "It might take me some time to find it."

"We'll wait," Elizabeth said.

That didn't sound like such a good idea to me. But I wasn't going to admit I was scared. Not in front of a girl. So I gritted my teeth and tried to sound tough.

"Yeah, we can wait," I told Mr. Hammersmith. "We have lots of time."

• • •

It was a good thing we had all that time, because Mr. Hammersmith spent a while in the back room. When he finally came out, he had a letter in his hand.

"Here's my proof. The Five Star Toy Company has been interested in my robot for a while now." He handed us the letter.

"See?" Mr. Hammersmith said. He sounded really happy to be proving us wrong. "Now why don't you two just get out of here?"

November 31

Dear Mr. Hammersmith,

Thank you for your submission of the plans for a robot that cleans kids' rooms. I think kids will love it. Our company is very interested in making the robots and selling them. Please let us know when you have a working model. I am sure we will all become very rich from your invention.

Sincerely,
Chip Modello, The Five Star Toy Company

That was weird. It sure seemed like Mr. Hammersmith could be guilty, the way he was sweating and acting all nervous. But this letter proved that Mr. Hammersmith had the idea before Leo. Which meant we were back to square one. We had no suspects. We had no motives. And worst of all, I had no best friend.

Elizabeth looked more closely at the letter. Suddenly, she gasped.

"This letter is a fake!" she said. "And I can prove it."

Chapter 14

"You can't prove anything," Mr. Hammersmith said.

Elizabeth ignored him. "Jack, look at the date on this letter. Do you see anything weird about it?"

"'November thirty-first . . .'" I read out loud.

"Exactly," Elizabeth said. "Remember the poem, Jack? 'Thirty days has September . . .'"

"'April, June, and *November*'!" I shouted. "There *is* no November thirty-first!"

"You were in a hurry when you printed out this letter back there, Mr. Hammersmith," Elizabeth told him. "You made a big mistake. A mistake no toy company executive would make on an official letter."

Mr. Hammersmith glared at us. More sweat dripped off his nose onto the floor. But this time it only landed on a box of nails.

Elizabeth wasn't giving in. "Hand over those plans," she demanded.

"Why should I?" Mr. Hammersmith said.

I was wondering the same thing. How were two kids going to get a grown-up to hand over anything?

"Because if you don't, we'll tell every kid in school what you did," Elizabeth answered. "And they'll tell their parents. Your business will be in big trouble."

Man, she was smart. I never would have thought of that.

"You wouldn't dare," he said. But he sounded like maybe he thought we would.

"*Wouldn't* we?" Elizabeth asked him.

Mr. Hammersmith looked from Elizabeth to me and back again. He was scared. *Of us!* Two third graders had just scared a grown-up. *How cool was that?*

"Fine," he said finally. "If I give you the plans, will you keep this a secret?"

"As long as you don't try to sell that robot anywhere," Elizabeth told him.

"Darn kids," Mr. Hammersmith muttered under his breath as he pulled the plans out of a drawer and handed them to Elizabeth.

Then he gave her a really, *really* mean look. Worse than any look I'd ever seen. Even Trevor had never looked that mean.

But Elizabeth just smiled and walked out of the store, with the plans in her hands.

Wow! Elizabeth was really keeping her cool.

Me? I was shaking in my sneakers. Any minute now I thought I might puke. But I held it back. I was pretty sure puking on the sidewalk wasn't something real detectives did.

My heart didn't stop pounding until I was three blocks away. I couldn't believe what had just happened.

"We did it!" I shouted.

"What did you do?" asked a squeaky voice. I looked up and saw Zippy and Zappy looking down at me from a tree branch.

"Not you again," I groaned.

"Who are you talking to?" Elizabeth looked up. "Oh. Those two cute little squirrels."

"They're not cute," I told her. "They're mean. They call me Big Head."

Elizabeth laughed.

"It's not funny," I told her.

"Ready. Aim. FIRE!" the squirrels squeaked.

"Let's get out of here!" I shouted.

Acorns blasted out of the tree. Elizabeth and I scrambled to get away.

"Wow! It's a good thing they didn't have anything bigger to throw at us," Elizabeth said. "Imagine if they were bouncing baseballs against our heads instead of acorns."

Bouncing balls.

Wow. Suddenly, I had a great idea. I knew exactly what I was going to do for the science fair.

"Thanks, you guys!" I called back to Zippy and Zappy. "You just solved my other problem."

"What problem?" Elizabeth asked me.

"My science project," I said. "I'm going to test what makes balls bounce. Like, do hard rubber balls bounce higher than soft ones?"

"And what about if a ball is frozen?" Elizabeth asked me. "Or hot? How will *that* make it bounce? And what about the size? And . . ."

Elizabeth was really getting into this. She even sounded impressed. Wow. I'd come up with a science project that the *Brainiac* liked. And I'd come up with it all by myself.

Boing. Another acorn whacked me in the head.

"Heads up!" Zappy shouted.

Okay, *almost* all by myself.

Still, I was pretty proud. Proud enough to feel like I deserved a double dip of chocolate chunk ice cream in a waffle cone. Which I would definitely get for myself—as soon as I was brave enough to go back to Pig Path Road. But that wasn't going to happen today. Even the thought of a double dip cone wasn't enough to make me want to risk seeing Mr. Hammersmith again so soon.

Chapter 15

"Apologize to Scout," I told Leo, when Elizabeth, Scout, and I brought his robot plans to his house.

"Why?" Leo asked. "It's not like he's going to understand me."

"He'll know you're saying something nice from your tone," Elizabeth said. Then she winked at me. *Oh man*. Why did she have to do that in front of Leo?

Luckily Leo didn't notice. He was too busy apologizing to Scout.

"Sorry, Scout."

Scout gave Leo a big, soggy dog lick on the nose.

"Yuck!" Leo said. "His breath smells gross."

"Not to other dogs," I told him.

"There's one thing I don't get," Leo said. "How did you two wind up doing this together?"

Uh-oh. Was Elizabeth going to spill my secret?

"Jack and I both like solving mysteries," she said.

Phew. Luckily, the Brainiac is good at keeping secrets.

She was also right about how we liked solving mysteries. Sure, the Brainiac was annoying, and it had *definitely* been scary talking to Mr. Hammersmith, but it had been exciting, too.

"We're in the detective business," I told Leo.

"You did a good job," Leo admitted. "But I still don't know how Mr. Hammersmith stole the plans without me noticing."

"Your hands were full of the supplies," I explained. "Mr. Hammersmith pretended to be slipping the instructions into your backpack. But he just gave you the receipt. You couldn't tell because you were wearing your backpack behind you." I smiled proudly. I'd figured out that part all by myself.

"I still can't believe Mr. Hammersmith stole my plans," Leo said.

Elizabeth shrugged. "That's the thing about mysteries. Sometimes the person who did it is the one you least expect."

I looked over at the Brainiac. *My partner.* I guess sometimes the person who helps you *solve* mysteries is the one you least expect, too.

"I'm glad Scout didn't know I blamed him," Leo said.

"How do you know he didn't?" I asked him.

"Come on," Leo said. "Dogs aren't that smart."

Not that smart? Was he kidding? If it hadn't been for Scout and his friends, Leo wouldn't have his plans for a science project at all.

But I didn't tell him that. Instead, I said, "You'd be surprised. Dogs are pretty smart. *Trust me.*"

CALLING ALL DETECTIVES!

Be sure to read all the Jack Gets a Clue mysteries!

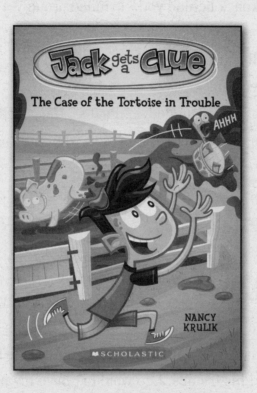

Here's a sneak peek of

The Case of the Tortoise in Trouble ...

Suddenly, I glanced down at my backpack. It was squirming in the bus seat next to me. I did a double take. Backpacks aren't supposed to move.

Weird.

"Hey! Who turned out the lights?"

Double weird. Backpacks don't talk, either.

But *animals* squirm. And they talk. At least to me. I reached into my bag and pulled out a very frightened tortoise.

"Mia!" I shouted angrily.

"Why did you bring Mia's tortoise?" Leo asked me.

"I didn't," I told him. "She must have shoved him in my backpack this morning."

Mrs. Sloane looked back to see what the commotion was about. "Jack! Why would you bring a tortoise on a school field trip?" she asked. She sounded angry. Not that I blamed her. I was angry, too.

"I didn't," I said.

Trevor started to laugh. "Uh, hello? You're holding a tortoise right now."

Everyone on the bus giggled.

Grrr . . . . Trevor can be such a jerk.

"Trevor does have a point," Mrs. Sloane told me. "Do you mind explaining this?"

"I didn't bring Tut on purpose," I insisted. "My sister must have snuck him into my backpack when I wasn't looking."

Luckily, Mrs. Sloane smiled. "I have a little sister, too," she said. "They can be pains sometimes."

Sometimes? Mia was a pain *all* the time. But I wasn't going to let her ruin my day.